E
R35

Diego's Wolf Pup Rescue

adapted by Christine Ricci   based on the original teleplay by Valerie Walsh

illustrated by Art Mawhinney

Simon Spotlight/Nick Jr.
New York   London   Toronto   Sydney

visit us at www.abdopublishing.com

Reinforced library bound edition published in 2009 by Spotlight, a division of ABDO Publishing Group, 8000 West 78th Street, Edina, Minnesota 55439. Published by agreement with Simon Spotlight, an imprint of Simon & Schuster Children's Publishing Division.

An imprint of Simon & Schuster Children's Publishing Division
1230 Avenue of the Americas, New York, NY 10020

Library of Congress Cataloging-in-Publication Data
This title was previously cataloged with the following information:
Ricci, Christine.
   Diego's wolf pup rescue / adapted by Christine Ricci ; illustrated by Art Mawhinney.
   p. cm. -- (Go, Diego, Go!; #1)
 "Based on the TV series Go, Diego, Go! as seen on Nick Jr."
 "Based on the original teleplay written by Valerie Walsh."
 Summary: Diego and Dora the Explorer rescues a wolf pup.
 [1. Wolves--Juvenile fiction. 2. Dora the Explorer (Fictitious character)--Juvenile fiction. 3. Rescues--Juvenile fiction. 4. Adventure and adventurers--Juvenile fiction.] I. Mawhinney, Art, ill. II. Go, Diego, Go! (Television program). III. Title. IV. Series.
[E]--dc22   2006299173

ISBN-13: 978-1-59961-432-8 (reinforced library bound edition)
ISBN-10: 1-59961-432-4 (reinforced library bound edition)

All Spotlight books have reinforced library binding and are
manufactured in the United States of America.

"We're Animal Rescuers!" shouted Diego as he slid down the pole from the Animal Rescue Center's observation platform.

"Animal Rescuers!" chanted his cousin Dora as she followed Diego down the pole.

Dora was visiting the Animal Rescue Center, and Diego had a special surprise for her.

"Watch this!" said Diego as he cupped his hand to his mouth and called, "Ah-ruff! Ah-ruff!"

Suddenly several maned wolf pups poked their heads out of the tall grass. *"Ah-ruff! Ah-ruff!"* they barked.

"Maned wolf pups!" said Dora excitedly. "What a great surprise!"

The pups playfully scampered over to Diego and Dora.
"They're so small!" giggled Dora as the pups climbed on her.
"And this one is the littlest," said Diego as he stroked the tiny pup's fur.

Just then Diego's sister Alicia arrived with Mommy Maned Wolf.
"Mommy Maned Wolf came to the Rescue Center to have her wolf
pups," Alicia explained.

Dora turned to Mommy Maned Wolf. "Your little pups are so cute.
And there are so many of them!"

"Maned wolves can have up to five pups at a time," Mommy Maned Wolf said proudly.

"How many pups are there?" asked Diego. "Let's count them."

Dora and Diego counted the wolf pups: one, two, three, four. Four maned wolf pups!

Mommy Maned Wolf gasped. "Only *four* maned wolf pups?" she asked. "But I have *five* pups! My littlest pup is missing!"

"Don't worry, Mommy Maned Wolf!" said Diego. "We're Animal Rescuers. We'll find your littlest pup."

Alicia decided to stay at the Animal Rescue Center to help Mommy Maned Wolf with the other pups. "Go, Animal Rescuers! Go!" she cheered as Diego and Dora ran off toward the Science Deck.

Diego and Dora ran over to their special camera, Click.
"Click can help us find the baby maned wolf," said Diego.

Click zoomed through the forest and found the little wolf pup.

"He's heading for the prickers and thorns!" said Diego, watching closely. "He could get hurt."

"We've got to rescue him!" said Dora.

"¡Al rescate!" shouted Diego. "To the rescue!"

Diego and Dora jumped on a zip cord and zoomed through the forest. They landed at a fork in the road. "Look!" said Diego. "There are prints on each path."

"But which ones belong to the baby maned wolf?" Dora asked.

Diego pulled out his Field Journal and scrolled to a picture of a maned wolf's paw print. "Which path has prints that look like these?" he asked.

"These prints match," exclaimed Dora as she pointed to the third path. "*¡Vámonos!* Let's go!"

The path led them to a river. Diego pulled out his spotting scope and located the wolf pup's prints on the far bank. "We need to get across this river to keep following the wolf pup's tracks," said Diego.

"I can help!" called out Rescue Pack.

"Me too!" chimed in Backpack.

Rescue Pack and Backpack worked together to help get Diego and Dora across the river. Rescue Pack transformed himself into a raft. Backpack gave them paddles and a life jacket.

After turning his vest into a second life jacket, Diego jumped into the raft next to Dora. They started to paddle down the river. Suddenly Diego noticed a river otter stuck in a whirlpool. "We have to rescue the river otter!" he shouted.

Diego threw a life preserver to the river otter, and the river otter scrambled onto it. Then Diego and Dora pulled the river otter to safety.

"Thanks for rescuing me," said the river otter.

"We're Animal Rescuers," replied Diego. "It's what we do!"

Once on shore Diego and Dora ran toward the prickers and thorns. But when they arrived, the little maned wolf was nowhere in sight. Diego cupped his hands to his ears to listen for the pup. Finally he heard a bark.

"Ah-ruff!"

"It sounds like he's in these bushes," said Diego.

Diego and Dora stretched up tall to see over the pricker and thorn bushes.

The little maned wolf was heading toward a sharp prickly bush!
"Stop, Baby Maned Wolf!" called Diego and Dora. "Stop!"
Baby Maned Wolf heard the warning and stopped right in front of the sharp prickly bush.

Diego and Dora ran over to the little wolf pup and knelt down next to him.

"Hi, Baby Maned Wolf!" Diego said. "We're Animal Rescuers! You're safe now!"

"Thanks for rescuing me," said Baby Maned Wolf. "I can't wait to see my Mommy and my brothers and sisters."

Back at the Animal Rescue Center, Mommy Maned Wolf nuzzled her littlest pup and made sure he wasn't hurt. Baby Maned Wolf was so happy to be with his family that he jumped into Diego's arms and gave him a big lick on the cheek.

Then Baby Maned Wolf curled up next to the other pups and fell fast asleep.

"*¡Misión cumplida!* Rescue complete!" whispered Diego. "That was a great animal adventure!"

Did you know?

The MANE event!

The maned wolf is called maned because it grows a mane of long black hair on its back.

A leg up!

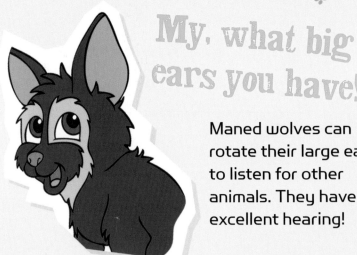

Maned wolves live in grasslands and swampy areas. The maned wolf's long legs allow it to see over tall grass.

Howl are you?

Maned wolves talk to each other by howling.

My, what big ears you have!

Maned wolves can rotate their large ears to listen for other animals. They have excellent hearing!

LG
3.3
0.5